Sleeper and Other Stories
Femdom Mind Control
Flash Fiction – Vol. 41

S.B.

Disclaimer

This is a work of fiction. Names, characters, business, events, and incidents are the products of the author's imagination. Any resemblance to actual persons, living or dead, or actual events is purely coincidental. All characters are over 18.

Table of Contents

The fun begins when you close your eyes.

Thank you to all patrons of Spell... B-O-U-N-D.

Friday Tease

Jonathan hated Friday the 13th. Everything about it gave him the creeps. As if it weren't bad enough to suffer the date every year, sometimes he had to multiply the feeling by three, and that was just an abomination.

"Why does it bother you so much?" His ex-girlfriend Becky once asked him, filled with good intentions that eventually backfired.

"It just does," he replied with a shrug. There was no actual reason for it other than that superstitions ran in the family and while he considered himself different from any close or distant relatives he knew, in some regards they were exactly the same.

"Have you ever had a truly unlucky event happen on such a date?"

"Not that I remember at the moment, but that changes nothing. It's still an ill-omened day and I'm not taking any chances, so I'm postponing our date."

"Please tell me you're joking."

"I'm not. I have to stay indoors until the day is over, otherwise..."

"Otherwise what? You just said nothing bad ever happened to you before..."

"For now, but who knows if this time it won't? I need to look after myself, don't you understand?"

No, she didn't, and patience for anything she deemed absurd was something she didn't possess either. Their relationship was inevitably strained following this conversation and ended faster than the devil could blink an eye.

Months passed, then a full year and Jonathan continued to dread the calendar more than he should. On the eve of the next Friday the 13th, he locked all the doors and windows, covered every mirror, hid all the sharp and pointy objects, and turned off every major electronic device. He would stay in bed all day and all night until it was safe to face the world again.

"Everything will be okay," he mumbled, repeating this sentence like a mantra as he lulled himself to sleep.

A couple of hours later, he woke up from a furious dream with a loud crash coming from the living room. It was half-past 4 am and the sun wouldn't be rising for another two hours. Trembling, he descended the main staircase to investigate, prized baseball bat in hand.

When he turned on the lights, he saw an unexpected mess. broken vases lay on the floor and there were claw marks on the carpet his mother had given him when he first moved to his place. Something had dropped through the chimney to wreak havoc, and it had bright yellow eyes.

The black cat was an adult but relatively small compared to others he had seen before. It was still big enough to almost give him a heart attack, though.

"Oh, fuck!" his superstitious soul screamed. "What are you doing here, furball? You're... you're not a witch in disguise, right?"

"Actually..." the proud beast purred, licking its right paw. The cat jumped on the sofa and stretched, exhaling a cloud of green smoke from its half-open mouth. Jonathan blinked as he covered his nose and gasped when the four-legged animal turned into a two-legged vixen with short black hair and razor-sharp fingernails that could easily slice bread. She was wearing a faux leather dress with fishnet stockings and platform ankle-high boots.

"Oh, my God! You are... you really are..."

"I definitely am," the newcomer crossed her legs. "My name is Magdalene, and you must be Jonathan. I heard a lot about you."

"You did?" he cocked his head, still holding the bat close to his chest.

"Of course, I did. You're famous, dear."

"Famous for what?"

"Few people lock themselves in their houses whenever a Friday the 13th arrives, dear. When I heard that someone as gullible as you existed, I knew I had to meet you. Sorry about the confusion. Let me fix that for you."

Magdalene snapped her fingers, every object she had disturbed, coming to life at her command. Jonathan stared in awe as the broken vases became whole again and the carpet fixed itself under his feet.

"This isn't happening," he thought.

"Trust me, it is," she replied inside his own mind.

"You... what? How are you doing that?"

"Witches can do a lot of things, dear, and even more so on a day like this. I know you believe it to be horrible, but it's actually the most magical time of the year.

He stood there, blank-eyed, unable to process the impossibilities all around. As if she had kept her former feline agility, Magdalene leaped from the sofa and landed right behind him, black lips kissing his right earlobe.

"I can see you're afraid of me," she said.

"Y-yes."

"But also curious. After what I've just shown you, you would love to know what else I can do, right?"

"If you're really inside my mind, you already know the answer."

"It's not the same as hearing you say it," she ground her breasts against his naked back. "Do you want a glimpse of what's coming or not?"

"Is it safe?"

"Only if you want it to be..." she grinned. "Well?"

"Show me then."

"You forgot the magic word, boy."

"Please show me what you mean, Magdalene."

"Much better."

She wrapped him in her arms. Dark images of pain and pleasure flooded his thoughts, and he saw himself at her feet, a black collar around his neck and a cat's tail sticking out of his ass. Magdalene was caressing the back of his neck with a riding crop as he stared helplessly at a vortex of black magic flame where no thoughts of independence could thrive.

"As you can see, I'm quite the mischievous bitch when I want to..." she declared.

"Hmm," he moaned, drifting along in the fantasy with a vacant smile on his lips.

"Interested?"

"Definitely tempted."

"That's a good start," she released him from her grasp and started floating above his head. "Keep those thoughts in mind until the next time we meet again."

"Huh? You're leaving so soon?"

"I must. I'm also quite the tease, Jonathan, but you'll know more about that once I return."

"And when will that be?"

"The next Friday the 13th, of course. In the meantime, dream of me. Bye."

The witch vanished in another cloud of green smoke. The last thing he saw that night was the shadow of a black cat running past him.

All alone again, he sighed, and sat on the floor, his cock so hard it would take at least half a day to return to its normal state. Things had just changed for the better and they would only grow wilder from there.

Jonathan loved Friday the 13th. Everything about it was great. When was the next one again?

Gone Missing

The sun shone brightly in the sky, kissing Helen's delicate skin as she jogged. It was a Saturday morning and the park closest to her house was still relatively empty, making it the perfect space for her exercise routine. Five laps around the inner perimeter usually sufficed, but she wanted more. She would squeeze another two and then head back for a quick shower. Smiling, she pushed through the familiar path one more time.

It was near the end of the fifth circuit she first noticed something was off. There was a brunette in her early twenties standing in the middle of the grass, her make-up ruined by a steady flow of tears. She was holding what looked like a leather collar in her right hand and couldn't stop shouting,

"Come back! Please come back. PLEASE!"

At first, Helen ignored her but, surprisingly, the farther she ran away from her screams the louder they rang in her ears. Momentarily losing concentration, she stopped halfway and doubled back to check up on her.

"I'm sorry, is everything okay?" she asked.

"No," the young woman replied, traces of black mascara running down her cheeks. "My Fido ran away, and I can't find him anywhere. Have you seen him?"

"You lost your dog? I'm so sorry to hear that. I've seen no dogs around here this morning, but I'm more than happy to help you look around. Can you tell me what he looks like or better yet, show me a picture if you have one with you?"

"Of course," the woman handed Helen her phone, revealing a slightly overweight man on his fours, a leather mask covering half of his face, and a furry tail sticking out of his ass.

"I'm sorry, what kind of sick joke is this? This isn't a dog."

"No joke at all, and I never said he was a dog," a dark smile crept on the stranger's crimson lips. "Fido is what I usually call all my hypnoslaves after they've been with me for a while, and I really loved this one. He was great. It's my fault for not locking his cage today, damn it!"

"Hypnosla... right... hm," Helen dropped the phone on the grass and prepared to make a run for it. "On second thought, I don't think I can help you at all, so if you'll excuse me..."

"Oh, please don't go," the woman reached for her right arm, grabbing it as if it were a commodity too precious to lose. "Whenever I'm down a pet, fate always brings me a new one. It's no coincidence you and I met today, I'm sure of it. I don't do a lot of girls, but you're pretty. How about you become my next toy, huh?"

"Let me go, you freak!"

"I hate it when people call me that! It's your turn, boys! She's coming with us."

"Suddenly, four men dressed in tracking suits emerged from the bushes along the park's main path, surrounding Helen without a sound. She didn't see the syringe one of them was holding but felt the sting, all the same, a dark fluid running through her veins as she fell unconscious to the ground. No one suspected foul play as she was taken across the field of green before disappearing inside a plateless black van.

Fido 22 remains at large, wandering around with no memory of where he's been or what happened to him. Fido 23's training is about to start.

Humiliating

Josh: Hello, Monica. Are you there?

Monica: Hello, Josh. Yes, I'm here. Do you need anything?

Josh: Well, I was wondering if we could have another session soon.

Monica: What do you mean 'another' if we've never had one? Please explain.

Josh: I'm serious here. Do you think it's possible?

Monica: Hmmm... depends on what you mean by 'soon'. Are you talking about right now?

Josh: Actually, yes. I understand this comes on short notice, but it's the weekend, I'm bored, and...

Monica: Say no more. Unfortunately, I can't tonight. There's a bit of a situation going on here.

Josh: Oh? I hope it's nothing serious. Can I do anything to help?

Monica: You're sweet, but no. I just have unexpected guests staying over, so I'll need to entertain them until they're ready to go to bed and when they do, it will probably be too late over there. You understand, right?

Josh: Of course, no problem. I'll leave you to your affairs. Have a good weekend, Monica.

Monica: Wait!

Josh: What is it?

Monica: Call me tomorrow at around this hour. I should be able to talk to you properly then. Deal?

Josh: Yes, Monica.

Monica: That's always the right answer. Until tomorrow.

The next day...

Josh: Monica? I'm here. Any chance for that session now? I have some wonderful ideas that would love to explore with you.

Monica: Hey, Josh. Thank you for reaching out again like I asked you to. I wish I could say the news are good, though.

Josh: You're busy again?

Monica: I'm afraid so, dear. The guests are still here, and it seems they need me more than ever tonight. I'm so sorry to disappoint you once more, but I'll make it up to you the moment the chance presents itself.

Josh: Please don't sweat it, okay? It's all good.

Monica: You're not angry at me?

Josh: That's impossible. A bit disappointed naturally because I wanted to spend some quality time with you but that's okay. We'll get another opportunity soon enough, I'm sure of it.

Monica: You're so sweet that I really hate letting you down. Can you call me again tomorrow to see what happens?

Josh: Sure. Same hour?

Monica: Give or take, yes. Thank you.

Josh: You're welcome. Good night, Monica.

Monica: Good night, Josh.

The next day...

Josh: Hey, Monica. I hope you're doing well. Ready when you are.

Monica: Hello, Josh. Forgive me, but I'm confused. Ready for what exactly?

Josh: Our session, of course. I'm hoping third time really is the charm.

Monica: I'm sorry, do you want another session today?

Josh: What do you mean, another? When did we…?

Monica: Yesterday, and the day before. I was surprised to see you go for two in a row, but I guess that means you loved it, right?

Josh: Now, I'm the one who's confused. There was no session, I'm sure of it. I wanted to ask you to try something involving...

Monica: ... public humiliation. You told me that before.

Josh: No, I didn't!

Monica: Of course you did. How else would I know it then? I'm a mind-controller, not a mind reader.

Josh: I.... What happened?

Monica: Well, I did say I had guests in the house and needed to entertain them, right. Enjoy.

Monica sent hornyjosh-part1.mp4

Monica sent hornyjosh-part2.mp4

Josh: I... hmmm... this is...

Monica: ... humiliating enough for you, sweetie, or are you convinced you can handle more?

Josh: I don't know what to say to that.

Monica: Say what you always say. Do you want to go deep for me again and surrender completely to my wishes?

Josh: Yes, Monica.

Monica: Do you want my guests to laugh at you like they did in the videos you just watched?

Josh: Yes, Monica.

Monica: And if I send the videos to your sisters afterward, will you be happy and even more excited than ever before?

Josh: Yes, Monica.

Monica: Good boy. Deeper and deeper, ready for my pleasure, which is all that matters to you. Last question, my dear pet... how many zucchini are in your fridge?

He would have regretted answering this one... if he remembered it.

Last Courtesy

Professor Walters entered his office at exactly 9:30 a.m., weary eyes unable to mask a terrible night's sleep. A throbbing headache clouded his thoughts. The forty-five-year-old Philosophy teacher was eager to have the semester end so he could enjoy a well-deserved vacation but, before that, he still had to endure three more weeks of self-absorbed students who came into his class to do anything but learn. After spending the first months of the year devising innovative strategies to keep them motivated using down-to-earth examples from the reality they were familiar with - all of which had failed! - he had simply given up and was now waiting for his next paycheck with bated breath. The bare minimum is all they deserved, so that's what he would do, hoping he didn't have to deal with any unpleasant surprises along the way.

Unfortunately for him, there was already one waiting, and her name was Debra Palmer. The daughter of a diplomat and a former lingerie model, she was a beautiful green-eyed blonde who had recently turned twenty and couldn't spend half an hour away from her phone no matter what. She was wearing a short blue dress with a plunging neckline as she sat behind his desk like she owned the place.

"Good morning, Professor," she smirked. "On time as always. We need to talk."

"If that's the case, you should have scheduled an appointment? What are you doing here, Miss Palmer, and how did you get inside a locked office?"

"There's no place on campus I can't get in, Professor," she replied, spinning a silver keyring on her right index finger.

"You're trespassing and sitting on my chair. This is the first and the last time I'll be courteous enough to ask you to leave before I call security."

"It's funny you mention courtesy for that's what brought me here today. This is also the first and the last time I'll bring this up, so you better listen carefully."

Debra moved the chair to the side to stretch her legs, her tantalizing naked feet on display. From her cleavage, she drew a small USB drive, and said, "I'm afraid your secret's out."

"What are you talking about?"

"I've hacked your computer and now I know all about your extra-curricular activities. I've seen the pics on your hard drive, know the dirty little things that make you tick. I'm also aware of what you did to some friends of mine when you couldn't keep it in your pants. Your love for hypnosis and brainwashing really got out of hand, huh?"

"Those are the dumbest accusations I've ever heard! Please spare yourself the ridicule and stop right now."

"It's too late for that. The evidence is right here with me and before you think about doing anything stupid, be advised that I have copies ready to be leaked should anything happen to me, so you have no choice but to do what I want.”

“And what is it that you want, you little bitch?” he growled.

“For you to mind your language, for starters. My silence is costly, Professor. If you want it, you’ll become my mindless bitch. I’ll do to you what you did to my friends and turn you into a husk for my entertainment. Simple, right? Refuse me and everything will be out before the end of the day, so don’t. I want to see you squirm.”

Professor Walters clenched his fists, blood boiling. She wasn’t bluffing and, for a fraction of a second, he actually respected her audacity.

“You’re not the air-headed bimbo I thought you were, Miss Palmer,” he declared.

“You’re not the first to make that mistake. Do we have an agreement?”

“It seems you leave me no choice.”

“Good. You will call me Mistress from now to get you in the proper mood to please me.”

“Don’t push your luck.”

“Don’t push yours!” she fiddled with his computer until the screen lit up with a mesh of animated monochromatic spirals, his weapon of choice for mind games, consensual or not. “Sit and let’s begin,” she commanded.

The older man complied, the inner workings of his brain hatching a new plan. He would play long enough for her to be distracted and then turn the tables. By the time she realized what he had done, she would already be on his knees sucking his cock and swallowing every drop of cum. "Just you wait and see, bitch. Just you wait and see..."

She never did. The hulk-sized dildo ramming his ass before the first class of the day is the last thing he remembers.

Nothing Worse

Francine sighed as she watched the elevator doors open and Wanda step out, as magnetic as ever in a tight black and blue skirt that turned her already enticing figure into a living, breathing weapon of mass destruction. There was nothing worse than having the boss's only daughter around the office. Francine hated the way she looked, the way she talked, the way she presented herself...

Oh, who the fuck was she trying to fool? Wanda was gorgeous, the most beautiful woman she had ever laid eyes on with her honey-blond hair, crystalline stare, and full red lips that were a constant invitation to sin. She was fucking hot and knew how to push her buttons better than anyone else. Being around her was a constant struggle against her other nature, the one that whispered she was a deity put on this Earth for her to worship, an embodied temptation that wouldn't rest until her thoughts and ideas were centered on the sole purpose of pleasing her for the rest of her natural life.

"Other nature?" Wanda scoffed, stopping by Francine's corner to give her a clear view of her bountiful ass. "Don't you mean the real one? You have no secrets from me, sweetie."

No! She meant... Yes! Wait... Hmmm, she didn't know for sure. It was so hard to focus when Wanda was in the room and that seductive pose pushing the papers atop her desk aside... Oh, God! How could anyone be so perfect?

Francine closed her legs, hands struggling to remain close to her chest instead of playing with her pussy. Deep inside her mind, she saw herself dripping like hot wax from a candle, each drop burning another piece of her already frail resistance.

"You seem a little uncomfortable, Francine. You've made quite the progress since the last time I triggered you, didn't you?"

"I... I don't know what you're talking about, Wanda. Your father is not around, so you may want to come back after lunch."

"Oh, but I didn't come here to see him. I miss my favorite hypno-slut and I know your mind misses me, too. Didn't you dream of me last night like I told you to?"

She... sure... whatever she said. Her vision was tunneling, the entire world turning into a spiraling blur from which there was no possible escape. In her dream, Francine had dropped to her knees to kiss the hot woman's ass while the rest of the staff took pictures and captured footage to publish online. It was wrong, a travesty of everything she believed in, but nothing more than a dream... just an erotically charged and out-of-control dream...

"No, I didn't," Francine blurted, every word burning her tongue with the power of lies. She pushed harder against the seat, surprised that the chair remained intact. "Why would I do that?"

"Because you're my little mindfucked slut, and you're still dreaming. Come on, you don't want to disappoint your loving audience, do you?."

Francine peeked above her dividing wall, a dozen of avid faces with phones on the ready, eagerly awaiting the humiliating spectacle they had been promised. It was just a dream. What could go wrong?"

"I must kneel," she heard herself saying, unable to control the suggestions flooding her brain and her pussy.

"Now, we're talking," Wanda chuckled, unleashing the full power of her juicy ass. "Polish my latex with your tongue until you disappear inside your own reflection. Do it, bitch!"

"Yes, Wanda. Thank you..."

"My pleasure. This never stops being fun."

Remnant

Tobias turned on the bathroom lights and stared at the figure standing by the farthest wall, hands on her hips demanding his attention. Melanie was back although one had to ask if she had ever left.

"You're not really here," he said as he washed his face.

"I'm not? Are you sure about that?" she retorted with a mischievous grin. She was dressed in black leather from head to toe that Friday morning just like the day he had regained his freedom. The heavy make-up on her eyes and lips gave the early thirties Asian-American a ghoulish appearance that had never seemed more appropriate. He sniggered and said,

"Yes. You're just the fragment of a memory I want to forget. Leave me alone!"

"I'm not a memory. I'm right here. I've always been here."

"Nice try." Tobias grabbed his toothbrush and threw it at the nightmarish leather-clad ex. It phased right through her before landing with a "thud" on the tiled floor. "You stopped being a part of my life a long time ago. Why do you insist on coming back?"

"I will not answer that. You already know why."

"No, I don't. You're an abomination that almost destroyed me, and yet you linger on. I hate you, Melanie. I hate you so fucking much!"

"So you keep saying, but there was a time when you loved me more than life itself, and those were the best days of your life. You should have never left, Toby. You'll never find someone as perfect as me."

"Lies, lies, and more lies!" Tobias slammed the bathroom mirror so hard it was a miracle it remained intact. "You messed with my head day and night. I lost my friends, family, and my job trying to please you all the time. If I'd stayed another minute, I'd probably be dead by now or be just a fucking husk. There's nothing perfect about you. There never was and there never will be."

"Stop blaming me for what happened between us, Toby. I only did what you asked me to do."

"No! You weaved those thoughts inside my brain. The drugs, the brainwashing, the constant confusion states... all part of your elaborate plan to convince me of things I never wanted to try or experience for myself. It was always your will speaking through my voice."

"And that's perfect. What can be better than having no control? Through me, you were able to experience the highest form of bliss and then you traded it for what? A boring, mundane life where every day feels the same and nothing exciting ever happens? That's not for you. If it were, you wouldn't be seeing me right now. Accept the truth, Toby. You need to be my thrall again."

"Never! You're the past and I'm looking at the future. I'm never coming back!"

"We'll see who's right in the end. See you soon, Toby."

The memory was gone from view, yet its echo remained, accompanying him on his way to work, during office hours, and during the return trip. The smell of Melanie's leather floated in the breeze and every shadow kissed by the sun had the shape of her boots bringing him to heel. It was getting harder by the second, but he would not give in. He would not be hers ever again.

Tobias went to sleep and did so in peace, nothing unusual hammering his thoughts... but when he woke up, the remnant of Melanie's presence smiled happily on his bed, a dangerous heel placed firmly against his chest.

"Not long now," she smirked. He averted his gaze and screamed.

Sleeper

The familiar message tone rang in Jessica's ears as she rode the bus to college. The second semester was almost over, and she had aced every exam thus far. She was sure to do it once more just as soon as she found out who was texting her.

Jessica reached for the pink smartphone in her purse, a single word flashing white on the dark screen.

SLEEP.

"No, not now," she mumbled, heart suddenly racing inside her chest. "Not..." Her right hand twitched and dropped heavily on her lap, eyes watering. No one noticed what happened, for no one ever did. She answered the incoming call with an emotionless expression on her face.

"Good morning," she said, forgoing the title "Mistress" because of being in a public place. Bridget's warm voice echoed in her wireless headphones with the intensity of a volcanic eruption.

"Good morning, my little slut. Are you deeply entranced for me?"

"Always."

"That's what I like to hear. Today is the big day, huh?"

"Yes, it is. I'm excited."

"As you should. What you do today will be the key to your future and mine as well. You want to please me, don't you?"

"That goes without question."

"Then tell me what you're supposed to do after you finish your exam but be discreet about it."

"I will talk to Mr. Hughes about you."

"And then what?"

"I'll make him see what he's been missing out on since you've been gone. It will be great."

"It sure will. Remember to be extra persuasive because if you fail me..."

"That will not happen."

"Good. Remain in trance until you receive my next text. Mistress will be waiting for her new slave."

The call went dead. Jessica stared expectantly at the screen, the single trigger delivering her to the real world once more.

AWAKE.

The History student blinked, the realization of what had happened still present in her mind. Bridget was her former roommate who had been kicked out of college three months earlier for daring to have sex in an open classroom for everyone to see. While she had been forbidden to ever enter the facilities again, there were other ways to accomplish that, and that's where the sleeper pet came in.

Jessica would help her enact her revenge on everyone responsible, whether she wanted it or not, but given the programming was working as intended, she would always want it.

Jessica let go of the phone, horrified, and aroused at what she had become. Thanks to her sabotage, two of her former mentors had already fallen under her spell and Mr. Hughes was next. After that, only the Principal would be left, but getting him to "cooperate" would not be an easy task.

The young woman exited the bus behind and walked the rest of the way to campus with her mission objectives firmly established in her psyche. She would remain fully focused on her exam foremost until the moment the phone triggered her again with yet another simple, yet irresistible command.

OBEY.

Always. All for Bridget, regardless of consequences. Everyone who wronged her would be soon eating shit off her booted feet.

Thinking Not Allowed

It was that time again when hypnotic magic happened in the bedroom, whether he was fully prepared for it or not. Dennis could barely keep his eyes open when Samantha was still wearing her transparent pink shirt, but now that she was down to her bra and panties, and about ready to lose the former, it was even harder to resist.

"Awww, someone is about to go deep for me," she purred, cupping her delicious bouncy breasts as if they were volleyballs ready for a match. "How far do you want to go tonight?"

"As far as you wish to take me," he mumbled, a speck of drool on his chin.

"Hmm, that's a risky proposition, boy. Are you sure you're up for the challenge?"

"I'm definitely up," he replied, brushing his cock against her tanned legs.

"That much is obvious, but aren't you ashamed of wanting sex all the time?"

"Only if you're ashamed of making me horny all the time, too."

"Touché," she declared, grinding her right hip against the tip of his tumescent member.

"Hmmm, yes please... more!"

"Not before I have my fun with you," she finally let go of the push-up bra and had him sniff the silky lace. "Do you like it?"

"It's wonderful..." he moaned.

"But not as wonderful as these, right? My boobs are so perfect, so intoxicating... whenever you gaze upon them, your subconscious knows it's the right time to let them take over. Feel your eyelids closing as the bliss of trance slowly envelops you once more. It's what my boobs want and, by extension, what you desperately need too.

"That's right, close your eyes for me now, but continue to see my boobs inside your mind. It is wrong to resist their power over your silly man's ideas and so you won't. In fact, you'll forget to think from now on... You will do this for me. You have no choice.

"Listen, sweetie. Whenever your brain kicks in, you get drained and confused, unsure of what's real and what's not, and you don't know how to process the whirlwind of contradictory emotions within you. That's because doing so is unnatural. Thinking is a higher activity of the brain, not suitable for the likes of you. You can't grasp something as complex. Only women and their glorious boobs are beyond such limitations. Men just obey. That's all they're good for. You'll obey me and my boobs without question. Tell me what your purpose in life is, my dear."

"To do as you say," he replied, his voice as distant as an echo emanating from the earth's core.

"When?"

"Always."

"Even if you're not in a trance?"

"Especially then. You are everything to me. Your boobs are my world."

"Hmm, yes... and to live within them is the best thing that has ever happened to you. Do you know the one thing that would be better than my boobs?"

"Is there even such a thing?" he asked, head slumping.

"Yes. If you had boobs as well. Do you still wish to go deeper?"

"I want whatever you want..."

"Good slave. My boobs are in your mind, smothering any attempt to resist these suggestions. You see them as clear as day, growing, expanding, becoming you... They are the oxygen you breathe, the life you crave. You've been branded by them to be reborn. Deeper... deeper... nothing but boobs... you'll be my big-breasted mimbo soon."

Dennis let out a sweet exhale of contentment, no thoughts, no nothing... Perfection was coming, beautiful and unstoppable. He would sink and obey.

Unusual Collection

Juliette stared in awe at a spectacle like no other. As a reporter working for the most prestigious magazine in all South America, she had met many people with strange collections, but socialite Willa Hopkins had them all beat. The top floor of her summer home was entirely reserved for a paradise of colorful spirals.

She had it all: matchboxes, napkins, stamps, towels, duffel bags, drawings, paintings, sculptures, CD cases, cutlery, perfume bottles... whatever she could find that had a representation of a spiral had to come to her place to be properly displayed. Entering the main room of her private exhibition was like finding a portal to a fantastic new dimension where everything was possible. While most of the spirals were static, the illusion of movement was always present, undulating ripples just below the threshold of consciousness. Juliette's mind drifted slightly as she observed the accumulated madness all around.

"How long have you been doing this?" she asked, sipping a glass of tangerine-flavored water.

"Oh, I started right after I moved here so it will be ten years next August," Willa replied, cigarette and lighter in hand. The metallic square object's surface was covered in a mesh of black spirals.

"That's impressive, Miss Hopkins, but it also seems a lot of work. There are so many items here. How do you keep up with all of them?"

"I have a catalog system, of course," Willa danced around a group of shelves to reach a small desk where a brightly lit laptop screen was the centerpiece. "I take pictures of every spiral I purchase and upload the descriptions to this program I devised. A copy of it is synchronized to my phone, so whenever I'm out shopping, I can always check if the item is in my collection or not. It has never failed me once."

"Wow! Do you know for sure how many you own?"

"Naturally," Willa fiddled with the keyboard. "The total number stands at 10037 with at least one hundred more joining them soon."

"That's a lot of money invested in this, isn't it?" Willa laid down the empty glass at the rightmost edge of the desk.

"Money has never been an issue on my side of the family, as you well know."

"But why spirals?"

"Why not?"

"It seems such a random thing to collect unless you have a hypnofetish or something."

"Maybe I do..." Willa winked.

"You're joking, right?"

"Why would I be? It's a fascinating kink and I love everything that fascinates me. I also love to surprise beautiful and elegant women like you with my collection.

Please don't tell me you have a prejudice against hypnofetishists."

"No prejudice at all, but I don't understand the draw, that's all."

"What better place to change your mind then? I've had a lot of fun around here over the years."

"What kind of fun are you talking about, Miss Hopkins?"

"Please, call me Willa. And isn't it obvious? The kind of fun that fries minds and has people begging for more, obviously! Do you want to play?"

"I'm not that kind of woman, so I pass. Can we go back to the interview now?"

"This is the interview, dear," Willa reached for a handful of gold and silver rings with engraved spirals on each one and waved them before her dark-blue eyes. "I'm afraid I must insist you give me a chance to prove my point."

"And I think this is all the time we have for today. Thank you for showing me your collection, Miss Hopkins, but I need to..."

"... drop deep?" Willa smirked. "Yes, I think you do. What did you think of the drink, my dear?"

"You..." Juliette tripped on herself, every muscle in her body getting heavier and heavier. She fell backward, glassy eyes facing the glass ceiling, which was also decorated with impressions of spirals, all coming down to greet her. Her host had wonderful plans for her, but she wouldn't remember a single one.

Weapon

Aria pinched herself to make sure she wasn't dreaming. Standing in her bedroom only a few inches away from one another were two identical copies of her, albeit wearing significantly different clothing. The version on the left sported a military outfit in shades of dark blue, while the one on the right looked stylish and clean in a white latex lab coat. Both exuded an undeniable magnetism contrary to her in her fluffy pink pajamas with etchings of white sheep on the chest and sleeves.

"What the...?" she muttered. "Is this a dream?"

"Not at all, soldier," Left-Aria said. "This may very well be the happiest moment of your otherwise pathetic and miserable existence provided you are willing to accept the honor we've prepared for you."

"I'm sorry, what?"

"Please forgive my companion," Right-Aria replied. "The world she hails from isn't known for the social skills of its people at all. Apologies for barging in, Aria, but we need to talk. The fabric of the Multiverse depends on it."

"Hmmm... multi-what?" Aria pinched herself again, leaving a painful red impression on the back of her right hand. "Who are you? How did you get in here? And why does it feel like I'm looking at a mirror right now?"

"Because you are..." Right-Aria replied. "Well, kind of. Are you familiar with the concept that countless universes exist and that they all run parallel to one another instead of just the one you live in? That's the Multiverse Theory, but unlike others that are based on wild speculation, this one is true. Both General Aria and I hail from two different realities that should have never met but, one day, the unthinkable happened..."

"My side came up with a new type of weapon..." Left-Aria said.

"... and mine created a way to temporarily pass from one universe to the other. That's why we're here."

"Do you honestly expect me to believe this crap?" Aria shrugged. "That makes no sense."

"If you have a better explanation, we're all ears, soldier," Right-Aria said.

"Will you please stop calling me that? I'm not a soldier and I don't want to be one. I also don't want you here, so go back to your multi-whatever and leave me alone. I need to get some sleep."

"We can't," Left-Aria retorted. "You're our best hope."

"Hope for what?"

"The weapon we've created is too powerful to stay in our universe. In the wrong hands, it can completely rewrite reality. It needs a guardian, one that will not abuse its power. We believe that someone is you."

"Excuse me?"

"The General speaks the truth," Right-Aria nodded. "When our worlds met, and I realized what his team had created, the implications were obvious. We've been scouring the multiverse ever since looking for a way to contain this and you're it. Of all the variants out there, you're the purest of us all. By entrusting this weapon to you, we are trying to preserve the balance of life across myriad worlds. We need you, Aria. Please help us."

"No! This is insane."

"General, please show her the weapon. We don't have much time."

Left-Aria reached for an inner pocket of her uniform, producing a bracelet-shaped object with three red gems in its center. If they were real rubies, they were the prettiest the original had ever seen. Aria was immediately drawn to it like a moth to a flame.

"It's so pretty. How is this a weapon?"

"Don't let its appearance fool you," Right-Aria said. "It has the power to control minds and the temptation to do so is enormous. Luckily, you're different from the rest. Your heart is pure. We know for sure you'll never betray our trust. Please, Aria, keep it safe for us."

Suddenly, the two replicas started phasing away, broken reflections of a journey reaching its end. The bracelet fell on Aria's bed. She blinked, and the images were gone, as if they had never been there, to begin with.

"What a fucking weird dream," she said to herself before falling on the pillows again and entering a dreamless sleep.

36

* * *

The next morning, she was woken up by her girlfriend who had just returned from a trip overseas. Megan's lips were sweet as honey, but the young flight attendant was more interested in the strange piece of jewelry resting at the foot of the bed.

"Where did you get this, babe? It's gorgeous! Can I put it on?" she asked.

Aria's face turned white at the unexpected realization it was all true, but she couldn't utter a single word. Time froze as her world fell apart.

You Are Great

This needs to be said, so let me do it for you.

You are great.

You are amazing.

You are the best.

All the things you say and do have purpose and meaning, and just because you don't always see it, that doesn't make it less true.

You are great.

You are amazing.

You are the best.

You are the most formidable person I've ever met because your dreams are still pure, and your ambition is real without being overblown.

You know that good things can only come to you through hard work and perseverance, so you roll up your sleeves and face each new day with a smile on your lips. When the universe seems to be against you is when you shine the brightest, recognizing the challenges ahead yet refusing to be perturbed by them. To rise above everything has always been your destiny, so you do it again, and again, and again.

You are great.

You are amazing.

You are the best.

While it's easy to write these things, accepting them is a different matter. Many people go through their existence, holding on to fleeting shadows and seeing themselves as one of them, too. They don't recognize their inner strength and limitless potential, sulking in every corner as if lamenting did them any good, but not you. You cry when you need to, but your tears do not define you. They are but stepping stones for greater achievements, and you embrace each one as they come.

You are great.

You are amazing.

You are the best.

Everything you think is a good thought.

Every idea you have is a good idea.

Every action you bring forth is the best action that could have ever been.

All your choices are good choices leading you to the best possible outcome, and that includes this one.

You've chosen to read this text even if you didn't know what to expect from it.

After the first couple of lines, you had the choice to back away, but decided to continue all the way down here.

Even now, you continue choosing to read some more by going deeper within these words.

In and out, in-between, up, and down... it's all the same, for good choices never stop being good.

You are great.

You are amazing.

You are the best.

You are good at everything you do, including going into a trance.

No one falls quicker than you.

No one goes deeper than you.

No one accepts the truth of these suggestions as easily as you.

Some may come close, but you remain at the top of your game and always in absolute control of your emotions and desires.

This happened yesterday.

This is happening right now.

This will happen tomorrow.

You are great.

You are amazing.

You are the best.

Everyone sees you for what you are and reflects your greatness of body, mind, and soul.

Whether you're home alone, hanging out with friends, or kneeling at the feet of your hypnotic goddess of choice, you are always perfect and whole.

You are great.

You are amazing.

You are the best.

Wake up when you're ready to remember this all the time.

You Want to Be a Pet

There are times in life when we're certain of what we want and others where confusion reigns and nothing feels right. When those moments hit, the best thing to do is to hold on to a single notion and work from there until everything becomes clear. I know you're troubled right now, unsure of what idea is best for you, so let me help you with that. There's something on my mind that fits yours perfectly and once I share it, I'm sure you'll agree. That thought is,

You want to be a pet.

You need to be a pet.

You will be a pet for me.

Yes, a pet. You can be a dog, maybe a cat, or something more unusual like a pony or a rabbit. The animal itself matters not but only the feelings evoked, and all of them are warm and pleasant, exactly the kind of thing you need. Let me prove that to you.

What do you think about when pets come to mind? I bet it's peace and contentment, open smiles, cuddles, and wagging tails. Seeing a pet walking down the street or running around the house is enough to energize you and lift your spirit out of the funk. Pets can do that and a lot more by simply being what they are. Most of the time, they live carefree existences dictated only by the sunrise and sunset, the needs of the stomach, and their owner's presence. It's so simple, and yet so fulfilling that it's unsurprising you desire it for yourself too.

To be a pet is to be loved and cared for.

To be a pet is to have the weight of stray thoughts taken away from you.

To be a pet is to rejoice every time I draw near.

Such wonders can't be denied and once the realization starts to bloom, you need to water it gently so that it never stops doing so, and here's how.

You want to be a pet.

You need to be a pet.

You will be a pet for me.

Hear those words in your mind now and repeat them for as long as you want.

Only through repetition can they become your own.

Only through repetition you can become mine.

Repeat them out loud as you see the future you wish to make present for the rest of your life.

Cuddling next to my feet...

Staring happily at my beautiful eyes as I offer you a treat...

Welcoming the leather collar by the door when I tell you it's time for a walk...

Never having to worry about human clothes again...

Such lovely realizations and so much more are yours for the taking if you simply open your mind.

Open it for my voice.

Open it for these mantras.

Open it time and time again.

You want what you've always wanted even if you needed me to make the announcement first. Now, we can say it together.

You want to be a pet.

You need to be a pet.

You will be a pet for me.

Good pets are easily trained.

Good pets are always obedient.

Good pets never whine or complain.

You want to be a pet.

You need to be a pet.

You will be a pet for me.

I said you would love this idea and now you do.

The things I say always come true as long as you trust in them, too.

Focus only on this promise of happiness as you mindlessly repeat...

You want to be a pet.

You need to be a pet.

You will be a pet for me.

Good. I'll be waiting for you when you're ready to go outside.

About the stories in this volume

The twelve pieces of flash fiction included in this book were written between May 6th, 2022, and May 20th, 2022, and first published on my Patreon page – https://www.patreon.com/sbspellbound - as part of the *Flash Fiction Friday* feature. Every Friday, I publish 3/4 new pieces of content which, after a while, are compiled to create the titles in this ongoing series. If you like this sort of content and wish to see more, please consider supporting my creativity. The complete information about the tales is listed below:

- **Friday Tease** - Jonathan is visited by a sexy witch on a Friday the 13th.
  (This piece was first published on the post "Flash Fiction Friday 2022 – Week 19", on May 13th, 2022 - https://www.patreon.com/posts/66395988)
- **Gone Missing** - Helen offers her assistance to find a lost pet, but things are not what they seem.
  (This piece was first published on the post "Flash Fiction Friday 2022 – Week 20", on May 20th, 2022 - https://www.patreon.com/posts/66687646)
- **Humiliating** - Josh wants to have another session with Monica but she seems to be too busy for him.
  (This piece was first published on the post "Flash Fiction Friday 2022 – Week 19", on May 13th, 2022 - https://www.patreon.com/posts/66395988)

- **Last Courtesy** - Debra blackmails her Philosophy teacher after discovering his dark hypnotic secrets.
(This piece was first published on the post "Flash Fiction Friday 2022 – Week 20", on May 20th, 2022 - https://www.patreon.com/posts/66687646)

- **Nothing Worse** - Wanda triggers Francine with her mesmerizing latex-clad ass.
(This piece was first published on the post "Flash Fiction Friday 2022 – Week 20", on May 20th, 2022 - https://www.patreon.com/posts/66687646)

- **Remnant** - Tobias keeps seeing a "ghost" of the woman that once brainwashed him into servitude.
(This piece was first published on the post "Flash Fiction Friday 2022 – Week 18", on May 6th, 2022 - https://www.patreon.com/posts/66100983)

- **Sleeper** - Jessica has two goals in life: to ace her exams and please her owner.
(This piece was first published on the post "Flash Fiction Friday 2022 – Week 19", on May 13th, 2022 - https://www.patreon.com/posts/66395988)

- **Thinking Not Allowed** - Samantha hypnotizes Dennis with her boobs, taking him deeper than ever before.
(This piece was first published on the post "Flash Fiction Friday 2022 – Week 20", on May 20th, 2022 - https://www.patreon.com/posts/66687646)

- **Unusual Collection** - Juliette interviews a socialite with a peculiar taste for spirals.

(This piece was first published on the post "Flash Fiction Friday 2022 – Week 18", on May 6th, 2022 - https://www.patreon.com/posts/66100983)

- **Weapon** - Aria is visited by two doppelgangers with a strange story to tell.
  (This piece was first published on the post "Flash Fiction Friday 2022 – Week 18", on May 6th, 2022 - https://www.patreon.com/posts/66100983)
- **You Are Great** - You are given a boost of (hypnotic) confidence to face every challenge imaginable.
  (This piece was first published on the post "Flash Fiction Friday 2022 – Week 19", on May 13th, 2022 - https://www.patreon.com/posts/66395988)
- **You Want to be a Pet** - A hypnotic woman convinces you of something you've always known to be true.
  (This piece was first published on the post "Flash Fiction Friday 2022 – Week 18", on May 6th, 2022 - https://www.patreon.com/posts/66100983)

About the author

S.B., Simple Being, middle name Creative. Writer and artist with a penchant for themes of Femdom Hypnosis and Mind Control. His thoughts are his own except when they're not.

Besides indulging himself in kinky delights, he loves his furry family of two (dogs), sci-fi and horror stories, and puns galore. He's also been writing a piece of erotic micro-fiction every single day since January 1st, 2016 and has no intention of stopping anytime soon.

Find out more and keep up with his latest extravaganzas by visiting and supporting his personal website, Spell... B-O-U-N-D.